A CHURCHMAN'S
CONFESSION

IRENE HARRINGTON

A Churchman's Confession

© 2016 by Irene Harrington

ISBN **978-0-692-74464-2**

Printed in the United States of America.

DEDICATION

This book is dedicated to my mother, Ms. Garfield Olivia Hailey. She is the one who inspired me to write about her past history. She was and still is a blessing to this world. Although life wasn't easy for her mom's family, God turned that situation around for their good.

Mom, you taught me to believe in things that seem to be impossible. What some people may call a mistake, God will show them that what He does is in His will. Mom, you have always put your trust in God. If I could only live a portion of my life as you do, I too can learn to lean and depend on Him for everything.

Thank you, Mom, for all you have been for us. Thank you for pressing on when it wasn't easy. Thank you for living a life that had no shame. Thank you for enduring the pain with a smile. Thank you for waiting on God for everything.

I love you so much, and I always will. ~ Irene

INTRODUCTION

"Have mercy upon me, O God" was the heart's cry of the main character, James. He was guilty of a serious crime. He wanted God to wash him thoroughly from his iniquity, and cleanse him from this terrible sin. The only one who knew of his wrongdoing was none other than God Almighty.

James wanted The Reverend and the congregation to forgive him too. A man who goes to church every Sunday and Wednesday night isn't necessarily a Christian. He is in the church, but is the church in him – that church that God will be looking for when He returns?

Proverbs 16:6 says, *"By mercy and truth iniquity is purged: and by the fear of the Lord men depart from evil."* James had to tell the truth if he wanted to be forgiven. He prayed to God for forgiveness, but he first had to confess and forgive himself.

Psalm 91:14-16 says, *"Because he hath set his love upon me, therefore will I deliver him: I will set him on high, because he hath known my name. He shall call upon me, and I will answer him: I will be with him in trouble; I will deliver him, and honor him, and show him my salvation."*

TABLE OF CONTENTS

FOREWORD

"If you are searching for answers about family values and unity, Irene Harrington writes with an incredible passion to demonstrate the importance of keeping the family united. In a world where family values are diminishing, Irene unleashes some inspiring words through a journey of memoirs and Christian principles that bridges the gap in keeping families united."

~ Gregory L. Everett, Senior Pastor
First Baptist Church of Wadesboro (NC)

Chapter One
Bloodstained Hands

FEBRUARY WAS COLD AND DREARY ON THIS HORRIFYING EVENING. As James hopped onto his homemade horse and buggy, his hands trembled with fear. His mind began to search for answers. *"Why did I do that? If Betsy tells on me, they're going to put me in jail for life. Oh my God! What about my family? If this gets out, it will hurt my children, my sisters and brothers."* His thoughts raced. *"I'm a terrible man! I don't deserve to live. I don't deserve my family. I should be locked up! What am I going to do?"* he cried.

As he rode down the one-lane dusty dirt road, sweat poured down his face. His eyes were bloodshot, like coals burning in a blazing fire. His hands and pants were stained with innocent blood – blood of a young'un who was blameless and couldn't protect herself.

As he grabbed his temple to ease the tension from his head, his imagination ran wild. He could still feel the girl's hands hitting and pushing him away. He could hear her screaming for help, but there was nobody to rescue her from the terrible beast within him. *"What in this world am I going to do?"* he screamed to himself. *"You got to get a hold of yourself. It's not as bad as you think. Mrs. Betsy wanted it to happen. She made you do it. That's why she called you to bring the wood. They didn't need wood this early. It was in her plan. God! Why did I do it?"* James rehearsed in his mind, over and over again.

The sun was going down. He passed the old county school. He passed the church he grew up in, then the cotton field his family owned for years. He stopped the buggy. Tears flowed down his beard. He reached for a handkerchief from his side pocket. He tried to wipe the tears from his face, but the more he wiped, the more his eyes over-flowed. He got out of the wagon, stared at his horse, and cried, *"I don't know, I don't know! God help me, I just don't know what to do."*

When he was almost at his house, he looked up and saw the bed-room lamp burning. A shadow of his wife stood near the window. She held the baby. *"Jimmy should be asleep by now,"* he thought. He took the horse and buggy to the barn that was behind the house. He tied the horse near the trough of hay that was left for food. He walked into the barn, took off his hat, and then his shirt and pants. He always kept extra clothes in the barn, in case of emergencies or a fire. He grabbed a pair of bib overalls, and put them on top of his underwear. As he walked out of the barn, his old hound dog licked his hands and jumped on him as he always did for attention. But this evening, James didn't even notice the dog. He didn't rub him or pat him on his back. He hung his arms down to his side and dropped his head in shame.

When he opened the door, Jimmy was standing near his mom

holding on to her night gown. "Why aren't y'all in bed?" James asked. "It was getting late and I didn't know where you was," said Mrs. Elisha. "What happened to your clothes? Did you get wet?" she asked. "No, I just wanted to change before I came inside," said James. Mrs. Elisha looked at James' face. Then she looked at his hands and down at his feet. "James," she said fearfully. "What's wrong with you? You don't look right, and I feel some kind of way inside," she said. James never looked up at Mrs. Elisha as she was talking to him. He hung his head.

"The Lord knows something is wrong with this man!" she murmured. "Do you want something to eat?" she asked. But James was as full as a hog that was ready for the kill. He knew in his heart what happened. He couldn't rest with the guilt and shame that was before him. *"It's going to get out. It's going to spread like wild fire. My pastor, my children, and all of my neighbors will know."* James pondered all these things in his heart. "If you're not going to eat, take a wash up and get ready for bed then," Mrs. Elisha demanded.

It was now 10 o'clock at night. James was still up, and he rocked in his old rocking chair. The squeaking of the old rocker woke Mrs. Elisha up. She walked to the kitchen where James was sitting. "Are you coming to bed, James?" asked Mrs. Elisha. "I will in a little bit," he said. Mrs. Elisha pulled a chair from the kitchen table to sit down. She looked at James. She put her hand on his knee and asked, "What is wrong with you? I have never seen you like this before. "I'll be all right, Elisha, you just go on to bed," said James. I'll be all right, just let me be for now."

Around midnight, James finally made it to his bedroom. When he got into bed, he rolled as far away from Mrs. Elisha as he could and turned his back to her. He tried to push the covers between the two of them. She tried to give him a hug and kiss him good night, but he acted as though he was dead sleep. He never turned from the wall that he was facing.

James got up the next morning. He had to go into town for some feed and seeds for the farm. He loaded the wagon with buckets and sacks for his supplies. He rode for about two miles, past neighbors who were picking cotton in fields and past homes of some of the church members. He greeted them as though nothing happened.

Finally, he arrived at his destination. He tied his horse to the post in front of the old general store. As he walked into the old general store, he saw Chesterfield's chief of police standing at the counter. "Good morning, James," said the Chief. "Good morning, sir," said James. James never looked at the Chief. He just hung his head as if everyone knew his horrible secret. He walked around the store and gathered what he needed for his farm.

"It's a shame what happened down there at Ol' Man Tom's home last night," the chief told the clerk. "I didn't hear," said the clerk.

"The old lady that married the man said somebody broke in the window and raped one of his daughters. They don't know who did it yet. It's a shame, you can't trust nobody these here days," said the chief.

When James checked out his goods, he left the store and didn't look back. As he rode out of town, his conscience whipped him to pieces. *"I can't go on like this. I used to be a praying man, and now I am a shamed man. I don't like this feeling. When everyone finds out that I did it, I will be the talk of this town. God, you just got to help me out of this mess,"* James prayed.

James rode into his barn and took all of his goods off the wagon.

He walked to the back of the barn where he kept his sacks of feed. He found an old chair buried under some of the hay that was thrown near the wall. He pulled out the chair and sat down. He fell asleep. Hours went by. Then morning came.

When he opened his eyes, his wife was standing in the doorway. The sun blinded him, so he couldn't see who she was. "Who is that?" he asked. "James, why are you in here?" asked Mrs. Elisha. "I thought something had happened to you. I was going to call the police this morning. You didn't come to bed last night. Did you sleep in here all night long?" she asked. James never looked up at her. "I'll be all right. I just got to get myself together," he said. "Get yourself together about what?" asked Mrs. Elisha. James never said another word. Mrs. Elisha walked out of the barn. She gathered her clothes in the tin tub and started hanging them on the line. Then she opened her mouth as wide as she could. "God, you got to show me something. God, please! God, let it be known, right now, oh right now, oh right now," she cried. Then she started humming a tune to herself. "Lord, you know what's wrong with that man, because you knows everything about your children, and you know what James has done, Lord. I'm going to trust you dear Lord with this!" said Mrs. Elisha.

James stood and watched his wife hanging the clothes on the line. *"I can't hide anything from her. It's like she can read my mind or something. I got to talk to somebody,"* he said to himself.

"I'm going to ride out for a bit, and I'll be back sometime this afternoon. You don't have to leave me any supper," James said. Mrs. Elisha looked over her shoulder at James and did not part her lips.

Six Weeks Later

Reverend Q.J. Hanns lived about four miles from James' house. He was an upright man of God. He did not sugar coat the Word. Whenever he gave the Word on Sunday morning, his members knew he was preaching nothing but the truth from God. If Reverend Hanns said it, then God told him to say it. "God's word is for God's people," Reverend Hanns would say during his sermons.

James arrived at Reverend Hanns' home. As he walked onto the porch, he turned and looked back to see if anyone was watching him. He knocked on the door. He heard a soft voice say, "Come in." It was The Reverend's wife, Mrs. Radie. James opened the door, and walked in. Reverend Hanns was sitting in a large chair near the fireplace. "Come on in, Deacon. What can I help you with this fine morning the Lord has made?" asked The Reverend. "Ah' Reverend, I would like to talk to you, alone please Sir," pleaded James. "Momma, would you please excuse deacon and me for a while? I believe he has something on his mind," said The Reverend to his wife. "Sure, I don't mind. How is the family, Brother James?" asked Mrs. Radie. "They doing pretty good," said James. "Thank you, Momma," said Reverend Hanns.

Mrs. Radie went outside to tend her flowers and feed the chickens.

"Have a seat, Deacon, and I will try to help you out this morning," said The Reverend. James looked around the room and grabbed one of chairs from the dining room table. He sat down near The Reverend. "Reverend, you know, I have tried to live a Christian life ever since the Lord called me to be a deacon. But, you know, the body gets weak sometimes. I know the Lord will forgive us if we ask him. I try to pray to God for forgiveness, and it just won't go any farther than from the bed post to the ceiling. I'm so troubled, I can't sleep at night. I get up and go out to the barn and cry. I need help, and I need prayer. I'm here to ask you to pray for me first, and then hear my story. I did a bad thing, and shame is about to consume me," James pleaded. Reverend Hanns looked at James. His forehead wrinkled with worry as he wondered what had made James so upset.

"Brother James, let's stop talking for a moment and have a word of prayer," said The Reverend. "Father God, once more You have given us this day. We want to first of all thank You for Your many blessings. You kept us all through the night. You didn't let anything or anybody hurt or harm us. Now, Lord, be with all of your people this morning. Whatever is on Brother James' mind this morning, ease his pain right now, Jesus. Show me Your way God, so I may do Your will. All these blessings we ask in Your name. Amen. Amen. Amen," said The Reverend. "Now, Brother James, I want you to explain to me what is going on, so we can pray about this thing," said The Reverend.

James looked down at his hands. Tears began to roll down his cheeks. He looked down at his feet, as his elbows rested on his knees. He shook his head and began to explain what happened on that terrible night at Ol' Man Tom's home.

"I did something stupid about two months ago. I can't live with myself, Reverend. Over and over in my head, I just can't seem to let it go," cried James. "Start from the beginning, Brother," said The Reverend. "It can't be that bad. You've been in the church for a long time. You know God's Word. When I hear you give your testimony on Wednesday nights, I have no doubt that every word of it is true. You're getting up in age now, Brother. There ain't too much we old boys have going on for us now. So, come on, start from the top," The Reverend said.

James asked The Reverend for a glass of water. Reverend Hanns went to the kitchen, and got a glass of water. He looked at his wife and shook his head in doubt. He walked back to the living room where James was sitting. "Here, Brother," The Reverend said. James took a swallow and put the glass on the floor. "Well, Reverend, do you know Mr. Tom who lives on the other side of town?" asked James. "Yes, Brother Tom lost his wife several years back," replied The Reverend. "You know he married again," said James. "He has five children and he needed help raising them. He took up with a woman named Betsy who moved here from a town in the eastern part of the state. She's pure evil, Reverend. I hate the day I laid my eyes on that woman. Anyways Reverend, she made a deal with me. I take that back. I allowed her to make a deal with me. I shouldn't have ever starting talking to that woman, but she fooled me, Reverend," explained James.

Reverend Hanns listened as James struggled to tell his story. But in his mind, James wasn't making good sense. "Brother James, listen to me. You got to stop beating around the brush. Just come on out with it. It can't be that bad," said The Reverend. James took another swallow of water. "I raped that oldest girl of Mr. Tom's! I did it! It was just like that woman put something on me. I went to that child as if she was a grown woman. I don't know what happened to me. I didn't mean to do that!" cried James.

The Reverend stared at James with his mouth wide open. He was at a loss for words. He was appalled to what he had just heard. "Brother James, did I hear you right? Did I hear you say, you raped a child? A child who cannot fend for herself! Are you telling me the truth, Brother?" whispered The Reverend.

James sat there, looking down at his feet with his fists under his chin. Tears began to roll down his face. Reverend Hanns got up from his chair. He reached for his Bible that was on the mantle. "You know, Brother, when we ordained you twenty years ago, I prayed that the Lord would send some good men to our church, 'cause we need good, respectful men in this neighborhood. I thought our church would be the temple where all of God's people could come and be safe from the wiles of the devil. All of the men who are deacons were appointed by my God. At least, I thought they were. I just don't know what else to say, Brother. This is going to be hard for the committee to come together on. I got to bring the board together on this one," said Reverend Hanns.

"When I heard about another brother stealing the church's money awhile back, I thought that was bad. He paid it back, and asked for forgiveness, and we went on with that. But, this, my brother! It's hard for me to believe. I just can't believe a man of your standards, doing a thing like that. Brother James, I want to ask you this. You said something about Mr. Tom's wife. She tricked you! How in the world did she trick you?" asked The Reverend.

James raised his head and looked at The Reverend. He took another swallow of water. "Well, Reverend, you know, I sell wood on the side," said James. "Some of my customers don't have money to pay me all the time. Mr. Tom goes to work early in the mornings, and his wife tends to the house and pays all the bills. I took them a load last month, and she didn't pay me for it. The first of this month, she walked up to me after church and said she needed me to bring out another load of wood. She said they were completely out of wood, and she wanted me to bring it that Wednesday morning. I told her that she never paid me for the last load I brought out. She told me to come to the house early, and she would pay me for the wood she got before, and the load I was going to bring. So, I went, but when I got there, she was standing in the door. She watched me unload the wood. Reverend, she had a look on her face like nothing I've ever seen before. I walked up to the porch. I spoke to her like a man should. When I looked again, she opened her night gown and showed me her breasts. I looked! I looked at her, Reverend! Then she opened her gown all the way down, and bless my soul, she didn't have anything under it. Reverend, you got to believe me! I asked her what in the name of God was she doing. She told me she was married, but if I wanted to get paid, she had something in the back room better than money. I knew it was a trick! I thought she was trying to get me in the house for herself, but it was the girl," said James.

James continued. "You know, Reverend, by that time, I was all aroused! My mind wasn't on the Lord, on the church, my wife, or my children. It wasn't on nothing but some devilment. So, I went into the house. Mrs. Betsy told me to come on and follow her. When I got to the room, there she was. She was beautiful, innocent, young and lovable. I lost it! It was like I was having an out-of-the-body experience. I went to that young girl. I can't get it out of my mind. She fought me, and told me to stop. I didn't, Reverend! I took that child! Now, I can't live with myself," said James.

Reverend Hanns listened intently as James told his story. He didn't know what to say. All of a sudden, The Reverend reached for James' hand. "Let's pray again, my brother. Father, once again, we coming to you, Lord. My brother, Your child has fallen, Lord. He needs You, Father. Lord, his conscience is whipping him, and the pain is getting worse, Jesus. I'm asking You to ease his pain and forgive him, for he has committed an unforgiveable sin to man, but man is not the judge, Lord, only You are. You rule over everything. You sit high, and look low. You know his heart. Please, Lord, let his evil deeds turn to good. Let this good be a blessing to You, Father. In Your Holy name we pray. Amen, amen, and amen," The Reverend prayed.

James opened his eyes. Reverend Hanns gave him a hug and shook his hand. "Brother, you have work to do now! Your first job is to tell your wife," insisted The Reverend. "Tell my wife? I can't tell my wife about this! She will never understand the way a man would, Reverend," said James. "Brother James, listen to me. You came to me with this. I did what you asked of me, and that was to go to God with you. I did what you and God required of me. You are going to tell your wife, and then you are going to tell that girl's father what you did. That's the only way to clear your mind. Telling the truth will set you free of this thing. You just better hope and pray that young girl isn't pregnant. My God, if she is, there's going to be trouble in this town. The sooner you do it, the better off you will be. If you need me to sit in with you and your wife, I will," continued Reverend Hanns.

James looked down at the floor. He put his hands in his pockets. "Well, you are right, Reverend. I'll try to tell my wife as soon as possible. If she dishonors me, then, I deserve it! I deserve anything she does to me. She may leave and take the children away from me, or she may forgive me! I just don't know which away this is going. You know, Reverend, it's been over a month already. In two more weeks, it will be two months. I haven't been back over there since that happened. I hope she is not carrying a child. I pray to God that she isn't!" cried James.

The Reverend removed the glass from the table that James drank from. He walked back to his chair, opened his bible, and said, "Brother

James, you remember one night you told the congregation that your favorite Psalm was Psalm 37?"

"Yes, I remember," replied James. "It says, 'Don't worry about the wicked or envy those who do wrong. For like grass, they soon fade away like the spring flowers, they shall soon wither.' That woman is wicked, and what she did to you was wrong. Her day is coming, you just wait and see. Don't nothing good come to women of her kind. You got to do what the Word says do. Trust in the Lord and do good, then you will live safely in the land and prosper. Do what the Lord wants you to do. Tell your wife and see what will happen. If she has the Lord in her like she said she does, then, she will forgive you, and you keep yourself only to her. If she doesn't forgive you, then you have done what the Lord has required of you. It will be out of your hands. Just pray for her, don't stop loving her, and the Lord will hear your prayer! Pray that the Lord let His will be done," Reverend Hanns said.

James walked out of the house. He turned and looked back at The Reverend. "Thank you, Reverend. Thank you for everything. Could I ask one more favor of you?" asked James. "Sure," replied The Reverend. "After I talk to my wife, will you please go with me to Mr. Tom's house? I need a little support, and you will be the right one to give me what I need," pleaded James. Reverend looked at James through the screen door and answered, "Yes, I will be happy to go with you, my brother."

Chapter Two
First Month

THE WIND BLEW THROUGH THE CLOTHES THAT WERE LEFT ON THE LINE OVERNIGHT. Clair sat on the porch waiting to fill the basket with the fresh-smelling wash from the day before. All of a sudden, she felt faint. She grabbed her stomach and threw up a big blob of gunk. She was sick to her stomach. She held her head over the balance of the porch. *"O God, what is wrong with me?"* she asked herself. Again, she vomited everything that was inside of her little frail body. *"What did I eat that made me sick?"* she wondered. She ran into the house. A glass of cold water sat on the table. She drank the water, and it came back up. *"Oh, my God! I feel like someone is turning me around and around. It won't stop!"* Clair cried. She walked to the bedroom and laid her head on the quilt that was at the foot of the bed. *"I'll be all right if I stay here for a while,"* she said to herself. Clair rolled back and forth on her stomach. She tried to ease the sickness that had attacked her body. Finally, she fell asleep.

Three hours passed when Clair rose up from the bed. *"How long have I been asleep?"* she thought to herself. She looked outside the window. Her daddy was leaving the house on his mule and wagon. She watched him until he was out of sight. All of a sudden, she heard Mrs. Betsy walking down their long hallway. Her footsteps were getting closer. "Gal, you finally got up off that there bed. Do you hear me talking to you?" she scolded Clair. "Yes, Mrs. Betsy. I was feeling sick a while ago, and then I fell asleep," Clair explained. "Did you get all the clothes off the line like I told you?" Mrs. Betsy demanded. Clair stood there for a moment. When she tried to walk to the door, she turned around and fell on the floor. Mrs. Betsy grabbed the collar of Clair's dress and pulled her to her feet. "What's wrong with you, gal? Are you playing around this morning? You trying to get out of doing the house work today? If you are, you are wrong. I don't care how sick you are, you will clean this house today," Mrs. Betsy said.

Clair opened her eyes. She walked out of the room, down the hall to the kitchen. She began to move chairs from the table so she could sweep the floor. Mrs. Betsy was cooking black-eyed peas and hog jowls for supper. The smell from the food gave Clair a stomach quiver. She was about to throw up on the floor. She grabbed her mouth and ran to the back door. "Oh, my God! What in the world is wrong with me? I got to tell Papa when he comes back," she said. She walked back into the house. By this time, there was nothing left in her stomach to throw up. She just gagged as she tried to sweep the floor.

About an hour later, Mr. Tom came in the house and saw Clair sitting at the table. "What's wrong with you, my lady?" he asked. "Pa, something bad is wrong! I keep getting sick to my stomach, and I don't know why," Clair explained. "Did you eat some of those berries I told you not to eat?" asked Mr. Tom. "No sir. I know they are not ripe yet. I didn't pick any of those berries, nor did I eat from the garden. I just don't feel right in my stomach," said Clair. "Well, we're going to let the doctor in town have a look at you on tomorrow. He'll be able to let us know what's going on," said Mr. Tom.

The next day, Mr. Tom told Mrs. Betsy to wake Clair up early, so he could take her to the doctor. "Ain't nothing wrong with that gal, Tom! You just want to waste good money that we need here in this house. You need to give her a purging, and see if that will make her better," said Mrs. Betsy. "I know what I need to do, Woman," said Mr. Tom. "It might be something bad going around. You don't know about children. I've had them ever since their ma died, and I know when something ain't right."

Mrs. Betsy stood with her arms folded, watching Mr. Tom and Clair. She took the corner of her apron and wiped the snuff off her mouth. She didn't say another word to Mr. Tom, but the look she gave him was enough to kill him! "We'll be back soon. Go on to the kitchen and don't let the food burn," he demanded.

The ride to the doctor took about an hour. When they got there, the doctor was examining another woman. The nurse asked Mr. Tom what was going on with Clair. "She's been complaining with her stomach, Ma'am," Mr. Tom said. "What has she been eating?" the nurse asked. "Well, Ma'am, I don't know for sure. I asked her, and she said nothing. I try to feed them right. I buy good food for my children, and what I don't buy, I plant in my garden," Mr. Tom said.

The nurse took Clair into one of the examining rooms. Then she asked Clair to take her clothes off. Clair did as the nurse asked her. "How old are you, young lady?" The nurse asked. Clair held her head down as she unbuttoned her dress. "I'm thirteen, Ma'am," Clair replied. The nurse wrote something on a sheet of paper. "Do you have a fellow?" she asked Clair. "No, Ma'am. I don't have a boyfriend, if that's what you mean," said Clair. Then the nurse listened to Clair's heartbeat and looked in her mouth. She checked her temperature, and then felt her neck on both sides. "I'm going to leave for a moment to get a cup. I want you to pee-pee in the cup and give it to me. After you do that, the doctor will be right with you," the nurse said.

Clair did what was asked of her. The doctor came in the room and gave Clair a strange look. "You told the nurse that you didn't have a sweetheart, but I want to know if you been messing around with some other boy," said the doctor. Clair looked at the doctor as if he was off in his head. "I don't have a boyfriend, sir. My papa don't allow me to go anywhere. All I do is, stay home, clean the house and wash clothes. I don't know of a boy where I live," said Clair. "Do you know what 'pregnant' is, child?" the doctor asked. "Pregnant? Meaning, when you go to the stomp and dig out the inside of it, and the baby comes out!" said Clair.

The doctor sat down in a chair near Clair. "Tell me something, child. Has some man, any man, take you to bed, or in the barn and ravish you? Do you understand what I am asking you? Please, tell me the truth, child. We need to know. Can you think of anybody that has put their hands on you where they're not supposed to? We need to know today," explained the doctor.

Clair sat with her hands in her lap. She thought about the time when the woodman came in their house. She thought about how funny it was to Mrs. Betsy, but Clair didn't like it at all.

"It was a time when the woodman came in my room. He made me do it. He made me! I didn't want to!" Clair cried. "He made you do what?" the doctor asked Clair. She looked at the doctor and said, "I tried to fight him off. I didn't want to do it, but Mrs. Betsy told him to come to my room. My papa wasn't home. I didn't tell anybody about it, 'cause I was scared. He hurt me! He put his hand over my mouth, and then he did it to me. I tried to fight him, but he was too heavy. I couldn't fight him. I didn't know what to do. Mrs. Betsy laughed at me. It wasn't funny at all. He hurt me so bad, and then he stopped. He left our house in a hurry. I didn't know what to do. I was scared to tell Papa!" wept Clair.

The doctor looked at Clair with tears in his eyes. "It's going to be all right, child. I know you didn't know what was going on, but this Mrs. Betsy and the woodman did. I'll have to tell your father what has happened to you. Before he comes in here, I have to tell you something. Look at me child! You are going to have a baby," said the doctor sadly. Clair looked at the doctor. She began to cry. "How did that happen, sir?" she asked. "It happened! When he got on top of you, he raped you. He put his private part in you. You do know what a private part is, don't you?" asked the doctor. "Well, I heard my papa say, private part. Sometimes he would say down below. I thought you just pee through there. I never knew that a girl could have a baby from down there too," said Clair.

The doctor looked at her and shook his head. He told Clair that she was about six weeks pregnant. "Let me get your papa in here. I have to tell him the news. Don't you worry about this, child! You didn't do anything wrong. Somebody did this to you and they are going to pay for it," said the doctor.

The doctor opened the door to the examining room. He asked Mr. Tom to come in and have a seat. He began to tell him that Clair was going to have a child. Mr. Tom had to sit down. He looked at Clair and said, "My lady, you have made your bed hard, and you have to lie in it, and it will be hard."

"Mr. Tom, your child was raped," said the doctor. She didn't do anything wrong. Somebody took advantage of her. This poor child didn't know what was going on with her. A young boy didn't do this! It was a grown man! He has to pay for what he's done. We got to talk to your wife and find out who this person is," said the doctor. "Yes, sir," said Mr. Tom.

Mr. Tom walked Clair to their wagon. He helped her up to the seat. "My lady, why didn't you tell me what happened to you?" Mr. Tom asked. Clair didn't say a word. "Do you hear me talking to you? I tried to raise you young'uns the best I know how. Your ma left us all alone. I didn't know how to talk to you girls the way a woman should talk to you. It's all my fault! You hear me, Lady?" Mr. Tom explained. Clair remained silent as she looked out at the fields while riding down the road. She closed her hands together and put them between her knees. All of a sudden Mr. Tom started singing one of his favorite church songs. "Over my head, I see trouble in the air. Over my head, I see trouble in the air. There must be a God somewhere," he sang until they got home. Clair looked up at Mr. Tom.

"Papa," she said in a soft voice. "I didn't do anything wrong. Why did this happen to me? I was in my room doing nothing, and then he came in and grabbed me! What was I to do? You told us not to talk back to old people, and I did just that. I didn't talk back. I did what you wanted me to do," said Clair.

"You remember, Pa, when we got in trouble with the neighbors down the road from us? You left us with Mrs. Ella Jane, and you told her if we didn't mind her, to take a brush broom to us. She had to beat Callan and Jasper, 'cause they were throwing rocks on top of the house. I remember, Pa," cried Clair.

Mr. Tom didn't say a word. He was stiff with shame. His body didn't move. He guided the horse with his arms resting on his legs. Clair looked at her father. Tears rolled down his cheeks like balls of sweat from a fever. Clair put her arm under his arm and lay on his shoulder. "It'll be all right, Pa," Clair said as they drove into the front yard.

Mr. Tom helped Clair off the wagon. He took her by the hand. Clair opened the door to the house and went inside. Mr. Tom sat down on the old wooden swing that was swinging on the porch. He called Clair to come back to the door. "Don't you worry about anything, my lady, we are going to get the man who did this to you. Just wait and see," said Mr. Tom.

Mrs. Betsy was in the bedroom listening to the conversation with her ear to the cracked opened door. She ran to the closet and grabbed her house coat. She took her dress off and slipped the coat on. Then she looked around the room for her bible. It was under a pile of old books that was stacked on the chifforobe near the bed. She sat down in Mr. Tom's old rocking chair as if she was studying the Word for the evening. "Tom, is that you coming in here?" she asked, as she looked down the hallway. "No, Mrs. Betsy, it's me, Clair." Mrs. Betsy peeped out the door. She watched Clair until she went to her room. "That gal and her pa is up to something. I don't know what it is, but it's something going on," Mrs. Betsy thought. She folded her house coat around her waist. She walked to the front porch where Mr. Tom was sitting. "Why you sitting out here, Tom?" asked Mrs. Betsy.

"I got some bad news today. I can't believe it! It just won't stick to this here brain of mine. Sometimes I think I'm dreaming. You know what Betsy, I got a feeling you know something about all of this," said Mr. Tom. "I talked to Clair on the way here. She said it happened here at the house. These children don't go anywhere without me or you. So, where were you at?" asked Mr. Tom.

Mr. Tom looked at Mrs. Betsy. She couldn't meet his glance. She turned her head as if she was looking for something on the walls. "Did you hear me talking to you, Woman? Where were you at when all of this happened? My lady told me the woodman came on to her, and you told him to go to her room. Is it true?" questioned Mr. Tom. Mrs. Betsy stood with a grin on her face. She never answered Mr. Tom. He walked out of the room and slammed the door. Mrs. Betsy opened the door and walked to the front room window to see what he was doing.

"Oh, my God! What in the world did that gal tell them? I got to think up something. I know! I will tell Tom that the woodman tried to come on to me, too. That's what I'll say. Just let him say another word to me about that," Mrs. Betsy thought.

Mrs. Betsy closed the curtain and ran back to her bedroom. She took off her house coat and got into bed. She pulled the covers over her shoulders as if she was gone to sleep for the night. Mr. Tom walked through the house in slow motion. He looked into the girls' room. He looked at the boys' bunks in the kitchen. He stood by the ice box, as tears rolled down his face. *"God, please show me what happened in this here house. I don't want to cause any harm to nobody, but please don't mess with my children. Nobody don't mess with my children,*

Lord. They're all I have," Tom prayed.

He walked into the bedroom. He sat on the bed and took off his shoes and socks. "Betsy, I know you are not sleep. I want you to turn over here and tell me what happened to Clair." Mrs. Betsy didn't move a muscle. "Did you hear what I said?" demanded Mr. Tom. All of a sudden, he grabbed Mrs. Betsy by the papers in her hair. "You gon' tell me, Woman, and you gon' tell me right now!" yelled Mr. Tom. Mrs. Betsy screamed and told Mr. Tom to let her go. But the more she screamed, the more Mr. Tom pulled. "Who came in here and raped my lady? Mrs. Betsy grabbed hold to Mr. Tom's hand so he wouldn't pull all of her hair out. "Turn me aloose Tom," cried Mrs. Betsy. But the more she screamed, the more he pulled. Finally, Mr. Tom let go of Mrs. Betsy's hair. He got off the bed. He turned and looked at Mrs. Betsy. "Was it James? Do you hear me talking to you?" yelled Mr. Tom. Mrs. Betsy didn't say a word. She just peeped at Mr. Tom with one eye on him and the other eye under the covers. "You don't have to say anything. You're not answering me for a reason, and that tells me a lot. In the morning, I'm gon' take a ride to his place and have a long talk with him," said Mr. Tom.

Mr. Tom got up early the next morning. He fed the cows and the chickens. He took the children to school and rode to James' house. Mrs. Elisha was putting out her wash. She looked back at the wagon as Mr. Tom passed her by. "Good morning, Ma'am! Is your husband at home?" Mr. Tom asked. "He's gone into town. May I help you with something, sir?" asked Mrs. Elisha. "No, Ma'am. I need to talk with him. I'll try to catch him in town," Mr. Tom replied. He politely tipped his hat and said, "Have a good day," to Mrs. Elisha.

Mr. Tom turned his wagon around and headed into town. This was going to be a long trip into town for Mr. Tom. He thought of what he was going to say to James when he saw him: *"Should I just go ahead and knock him in his mouth, or should I start talking about what he did to my child?"* Over and over again, his mind played tricks with him.

Mr. Tom spotted James coming out of the Feed and Seed store. He rode his horse and buggy to the mounting post. "James! How you do there?" asked Mr. Tom. James looked back and asked, "How you do there?" Mr. Tom said, "I need to talk to you about a matter, if you please. There's a problem me and my family is having, and I believe you can help with it. You bought wood out at my place about two months ago, and I didn't tell you to. What I need for you to tell me, who told you to come out that evening?" asked Mr. Tom. James looked down at the ground while Mr. Tom was talking. He took his hat off and began scratching his head. "You do remember the day I'm talking about, don't you?" asked Mr. Tom.

"I remember the day. I think your wife sent for me to come out. She told me that you wanted to have enough wood at the house, 'cause you was afraid it would come up a big snow that week. I brought the wood out. Yes, sir. I remember that day. Is anything wrong with it?" James asked, as he watched Mr. Tom stare at him. Mr. Tom looked at James dead in his eyes, and asked, "Don't you go to church over there where Reverend Hanns preach at?" "Yes, sir, I do," replied James. "We got to go see him!" said Mr. Tom. "Somebody told me you're his head deacon. I try to live right in this world. I don't go around looking for trouble from nobody. I mind my own business and try to raise my children the right way. But somebody, between you and my wife, got to tell the truth about what happened at my place. You want to tell me now, or do you want to wait until tomorrow evening?" Mr. Tom asked. "I rather wait until tomorrow," said James. "Wednesday night prayer meeting will be a better time for all of us. I know I do wrong. Ain't none of us perfect! I kinda know a little bit about what you are saying there, but I been praying about that thing, and The Reverend been praying for me too. Yes sir, we will wait until tomorrow. I'm glad you stopped me, Mr. Tom. I've been wanting to get this here thing over with. I'll talk to you more about it tomorrow with The Reverend," James added.

Mr. Tom stood beside James with his hands in his pockets. He looked up at the sky as if he was wondering what was going to come out of James' mouth next. He did all he could to hold his peace. He knew from the conversation they were having, James was guilty. Mr. Tom was a good Christian man, a man who respected everybody and loved his family. He didn't hold any offices in the church, and he didn't go to church every Sunday, but he was a man of his word, and everybody who knew him could depend on him to do what he said he would do.

"All right, I'll be there tomorrow at seven thirty on the dot," said Mr. Tom as he got on his wagon. James walked over to his wagon. Then the two men went their separate ways.

Mr. Tom arrived home about an hour later. He took his horse and wagon to the barn. Mrs. Betsy was standing in the kitchen. As he walked into the house, she ran to the front door to greet him. "Are you hungry, Tom?" she asked quietly. "No, I'm not hungry. Where are the girls?" he asked. Mrs. Betsy turned around to go to the kitchen and said, "They are somewhere around here. I asked Clair to take the clothes off the line, but she just looked at me, and said nothing."

Mr. Tom went on the back porch and got the tin tub. He heated a kettle of water on the stove. He sat at the table while the water was heating. He put his arms on the table and laid his head down. *"Lord, I want to do what's right. Just show me what I have done wrong, Lord. I try to raise my children the way You will have me to do, Father. In Your Word, You say forgive, but where do I draw the lines? Show me, Lord, some way and somehow. I know you are not a God of mistakes, and You are not a God that lies. Show me, Lord what to do. I'm asking You in the name of the Father, the Son, and the Blessed Holy Ghost. Amen Jesus. Amen Lord,"* Tom prayed.

He got up from the table and went to his bedroom. He took his clothes off to get himself ready for a bath. Mrs. Betsy walked in the room and said, "Do you want me to wash your back, Tom? I'll get your soap and towel. Why you not talking to me?" Mr. Tom didn't have words to say. He just continued to wash himself and did not say a word.

Later that night, Mrs. Betsy came to the bedroom. Mr. Tom was lying down with both pillows under his head. He looked at Mrs. Betsy and said, "You know, I saw James today in town. We had a long talk about him coming to this house to bring wood. You know more about that day, but you don't want to say. We got a meeting with his pastor on Wednesday night. If I find out you had anything to do with him coming here, you know what's going to happen. I can't live like this. I married you to love you and in return, you was to love my children, just like they were your own flesh and blood. So, if you have anything you need to tell me, you better do it now." Mrs. Betsy stood over the bed and looked down at Mr. Tom with a sneaky smile on her face. She got into bed. Mr. Tom gave her a pillow and turned his face to the wall.

Mr. Tom got up early on Wednesday morning. He got his bible and went outside on the swing. He opened his bible to 2 Corinthians, one of his favorite books in the bible. "Be joyful. Grow to maturity. Encourage each other. Live in harmony and peace. Then the God of love and peace will be with you. Greet one another with Christian love." Mr. Tom closed his bible. *"Lord, you have spoken to me. I know You know me, and I know You. You don't make no mistakes. You have showed me what to do, and you have given me words to say. I will do Your will Lord. Amen, amen, amen."*

Mr. Tom took the children to school. He came back home to do his daily chores. Mrs. Betsy was getting dressed to go into town. "I'll be back sometime today, Tom," she said spitefully. Mr. Tom just looked at her and didn't say a word. He went into the house and began to sweep the floors and wash the morning dishes. As he walked into his bedroom, he saw the chifforobe drawers open. He looked inside to find Mrs. Betsy's clothes were gone.

"Oh, so she's trying to think ahead of me!" thought Tom. *"She thinks I'm going to tell her to get out! She knows the truth. She knows exactly what James is going to tell me. But, Lord, I'm going to beat her at her own game. I'm not going to put her out. I'm going to do what is right. I'm going to forgive her, keep on loving her, and treat her with the highest respect, and then, that will heap coals of fire on her head. She won't be able to take me being nice to her. The devil don't like it when you're kind to the ones who do you wrong. Lord, you're going to fix all of this! Just give me the strength to endure this thing."*

Seven o'clock Wednesday Night Prayer Service

James arrived early, and so did The Reverend. Mr. Tom arrived at seven thirty, and walked in the side door. "Come on in, Brother Tom. You should have come through the front door like all the rest of us," said The Reverend. "I'm all right, Pastor. I haven't been in a while, so I felt like it would be wrong for me to come to God's house through the front door under the cross. I just don't feel worthy to walk down the aisles in this holy place. You all sure keep the church looking good inside," continued Mr. Tom.

The Reverend and James were sitting at the front of the church. There were several other members there too. Mr. Tom sat down on the second pew from the front. He spoke to all the members, and took off his hat. Reverend Hanns opened the service with a prayer and one of the women sang a hymn. Reverend Hanns knew that James loved to read the Psalms, so he decided to study the Psalms that evening. This would break the ice a little between the two men. But what he didn't know was, Mr. Tom was already prayed up. God had put peace in his heart, and he feared no man.

"Let's all bow our heads in a word of prayer before we go any further, brothers and sisters," said The Reverend. "Lord, I want to thank you for this day. Thank you for waking us up early this morning. You didn't have to do any of this, Lord, but You did, and for that, I want to say thank You. Remember the sick this evening, Lord. Remember the ones in the hospital and the rest homes, Jesus. Remember the heavy hearts right now, Lord Jesus. And Lord, please remember our friends and loved ones, as well as our enemies, Jesus. Teach us to love one another as we should. Come in this place right now, Lord, and if any men or women got hatred in their hearts, rebuke it right now, Jesus. Take care of us in this place, as we continue with our Bible study this night. I'm asking you in Your Holy name. Amen," The Reverend prayed with one eye closed and the other eye on Brother Tom.

Reverend Hanns opened his bible to the 37th Psalms. "Brother James, will you please start reading the first verse of Psalms 37?" The Reverend asked. James began to read, "Don't worry about the wicked." He raised his head and looked around to see if everyone was looking at him or looking in their bibles. "Or envy those who do wrong." He dropped his hat on the floor and reached down to get it. "For like grass, they soon fade away. Like spring flowers, they soon wither." The Reverend watched James as he read the scripture, and said, "Stop right there, Brother. Let us discuss those two verses for a moment." The Reverend looked around the room. There were seven women there and about ten men, including The Reverend. "I want someone to define 'wicked' for me. Just tell me in your own words, what is a wicked person? Anybody," said The Reverend. Mrs. Annabell, one of the church mothers, raised her hand. "Well Pastor, I believe a wicked person is a person who will do most anything. That person don't care about nothing – his children, momma, daddy, his home, his neighbors, his church, and even himself. And when I say him that can mean a woman, too!" The Reverend nodded in agreement.

Then another mother of the church raised her hand. "I feel like this here, Pastor. A person who is wicked don't love God. You see, the bible said 'don't worry.' It mean just that. Don't worry 'cause God's going to get them for what they do. I don't mess around with such people. I don't want them round me, 'cause you don't know what they gon' do.

I remember when I was a little girl, my pa told me about a man who lived in the same town we lived in. He was a wicked man. My pa said that man didn't care about nothing. Pa said he cursed the sun and moon one night. He even killed one of his own children. He and his wife had two children, and he didn't want any more children. When his wife had the baby that night, this man took the baby from its momma and buried it in their back yard. Now, you know that was wicked. He was the devil's best friend, if you ask me."

The Reverend stood as she spoke. He watched the other members' expression. Everyone had their eyes on this woman. Some shook their heads. Some made comments by saying it was a shame, and others were speechless. "Well, you all are right. The bible also goes on to say don't envy these people," said The Reverend. "We don't have to lose any sleep because of these people. Don't get angry with them either. God will get them for all they do. He is sitting high and looking low. God sees everything. He's going to crush them like the winter leaves on the ground. Now, that don't mean the person is going to be physically crushed. It means ain't nothing going to go right in his life until he repent and get the Holy Ghost. That's God's word for God's people," The Reverend said.

"Brother James, keep on reading until I tell you to stop," asked The Reverend. Brother James continued to read, "Trust in the Lord and do good, then you will live safely in the land and prosper." Brother James raised his head and looked around the room again. The Reverend added, "Now, I want you all to pay close attention to what this brother just read. The bible said, to trust in the Lord. It didn't say trust in man. It didn't say trust in your wife, your children, your animals on your farm, nor did it say trust in your friends. You got to trust God in everything you do. When trouble comes, don't trust nobody but God. Trouble will come to all of us. What you going to do when it comes? You got to fall down on your knees and give it to God. He's the only one who will help you. But, if you don't do it, your life will be full of hell. You will be tormented in your home, on the job, with your family. You got to repent," said The Reverend. Everyone in bible study agreed by whispering to each other and nodding their heads. One woman who was sitting near Brother James raised her hand and said, "I don't do wicked things, and I don't like people who do. I don't want them at my house, near my family, and Lord knows I don't want them in my church. Some folks will play church up in here, and then they go out these four walls and do any God forbidden thing. I can look those devils right in their eyes, and tell they ain't no good. I know the Lord will forgive us for anything if we ask, but if the devil can do his thing to me and ask for forgiveness, then I'll do what I have to do to them, and ask for forgiveness too. Don't mess with me, and think you going to get away with it! God knows all of our hearts."

Brother James held his head down as though he was looking for something under the pew. "Reverend Hanns, I think I should go. It's getting late and I need to do some work around the house before I go to bed," said James. The Reverend looked at James and decided to go on with bible study, but he wanted to tell the prayer warriors about Brother James' problem so they could pray for him. "Wait a minute, Brother. Members, we have a serious problem with one of our members. He really needs prayer tonight. Brother James, do you want me to start from the beginning?" asked The Reverend. James stood in the aisle near one of the church mothers. She looked up at James, and then she looked at The Reverend. "What's going on, Pastor?" the woman asked. The Reverend asked James to sit back down. "All of you know our brother here. He has a serious problem. He came here tonight for prayer and asked for forgiveness from God and the church. You see, the devil will have his way with us if we allow him to. We all get weak sometimes," explained The Reverend. One of the mothers took her glasses off and folder her arms. She stared at The Reverend and then at James. "Reverend, you need to stop beating around the brush and tell us what's going on here!" the woman demanded. Everyone was talking amongst themselves, trying to figure out the problem before they heard anything from The Reverend. James took his seat, and laid his head on the back of the pew that was in front of him.

"This brother has gotten himself in a world of trouble. You all know he has a business on the side. He sells wood to most of the people here in town. Well, he was tricked by the devil himself! You know Mr. Tom who lives about two miles outside of town? He married a woman from another county, I think in the eastern part of the state. Well, she tried to come on to Brother James one night. She tricked him to come to the house, and Mr. Tom wasn't home. That devil in her didn't pay our dear brother here, and offered him the man's daughter for sex. I tell you, I just don't know what came over our brother here. She must have something going on with her, like working witch craft or roots on folks, because our brother here is a churchgoing man. I can't see him just going to that child on his own will," said The Reverend.

Another mother in the church stood up where she was sitting and said, "Wait a minute! You mean it was a child this here man had sex with? I know the family. Mr. Tom's wife was my friend before she passed. We used to pick cotton together. I know their children. The oldest girl Clair is only about thirteen years old. I know this man didn't have sex with that child!" the woman argued.

Everybody was talking and whispering about what they had just heard. Some of the women got up and threatened to leave bible study. Some said to put him out of the church. Others said they couldn't believe what they had just heard. The Reverend pleaded for them to sit down and come to order, but the more he tried to calm them, the louder they got. Finally, The Reverend took a straight chair that was standing near the heater and slammed it in the floor. "I mean for everybody to get quiet in here! Now, we know the problem. This man needs help. It could have happened to any one of us," said The Reverend. "Pastor, I don't mean no harm, but you are wrong," said one woman. "It could have happened to some of you men in here, 'cause some of you are weak anyhow! I watch you men on Sunday morning. Just let some young gal come up in here with a dress above her knees, and you will fall over one of them chairs trying to see. I don't know what you looking for! I know Mr. Tom's wife. Her name is Betsy. She didn't put nothing on James. He did just what he wanted to do. You all pray for him and let him go. Take him off all his duties at this church, because he ain't worthy. And if you don't Pastor, this here church will suffer for it," added the woman. The Reverend was getting upset. As the woman was speaking, Reverend Hanns opened his bible to Psalms 37 and the eighth verse. "I would like for all of you to sit down for a minute. We all are getting out of hand. This verse says; 'Stop being angry! Turn from your rage! Do not lose your temper. It only leads to harm.'"

"Brothers and sisters, let's pray for our brother," said The Reverend. "Let's not be angry at this man of God. I know men are different from you women. We do fall, but God will bring us back up, and sometimes this makes us better men." Another woman stood with her hands on her hips and said, "If you go on down a little further Pastor, verse ten says; 'soon the wicked will disappear. Though you look for them, they will be gone.' So I say be gone, devil! You need to get up out of here, 'cause you ain't worthy to be trying to tell us church folks nothing. God don't like your dirty deeds, and we don't either." The Reverend's mouth flew open. He didn't have words to say. Everybody in bible study was in a rage. The women talked amongst themselves. They wanted to get rid of the Pastor, because they thought he was being biased. But he wasn't for what James did, he just wanted to pray for the man so he could go on with his life.

The Reverend finally got everybody's attention and said, "Listen to me for a minute, people. Have you forgotten where you are? You all are in God's house. And God's house is not a house of confusion. We are supposed to pray for the sinner man. God loves all of us, and He hates the sin. Do you understand what I'm trying to say? The sin is what's wrong here! We all have sinned, haven't we, Sister Laura?" Sister Laura was sitting on the second pew where The Reverend was standing. She grabbed her pocket book. She opened it to see if she had some tissue for her nose. "Why you calling me out, Reverend? I ain't the one who did something wrong up in here. Just because James is a man, you men want to take sides with him. So don't put me in this mess," sister Laura said. Reverend Hanns took off his glasses. He looked at Sister Laura, and said, "You know, I was in sin once. No, I take that back. I was in sin a lot. I remember when I started preaching, the women tried all they could to turn me away from God. I know this woman. I'm not going to call any names, because that's what the devil wants me to do. But this woman came to my house one night. It was late, too. She told me that she left her pocketbook in the church, and she wanted me to go with her to get it. I got up out of my bed. I didn't know the devil was playing a trick with me. But I got out of bed with my wife, put on my clothes, and followed this woman to church. When we got to the church, there was no lights out here then, I got off my wagon and unlocked the door of the church. I had to go a good ways to turn the lights on. And do you know what happened? That woman grabbed me in my front. She rubbed me where I didn't want her to. What was I to do? I was a young preacher. I had just started preaching at this church. I didn't know these young devils in this neighborhood! That night, I gave in to the devil. We made love right here in this church. When we got up, she ran out the door. I got a hold of myself, and thought 'what in the world did you do?' I had to pray, y'all! You have no idea how I felt that night. I was ashamed. I was a sinner man, standing in here, trying to tell God's people how to live. I promised my God I would never let the devil grab me like that again. And I didn't y'all! The only woman who grabs me now is my wife. But it took prayer, brothers and sisters."

Sister Laura looked at the preacher so hard that she trembled in her seat. She put her pocketbook across her stomach. She crossed her legs. She tugged at her dress tail. She put her hand over her mouth, and held her head down to her breast. She got up and stared at The Reverend and said, "I've had enough of this church and the crooked men in here. I'm leaving." She grabbed her purse and walked to the entrance door. She gave The Reverend one final look, as if she was asking 'why did you tell that?'

Everyone looked at Sister Laura as she walked out the church. One of the men stood up and said, "Pastor, you are right, and we are the ones wrong. We need to hear from Brother James. Let him confess his sins to God and ask for forgiveness. I've been there, Pastor. I know what you went through when you first started out. I ain't no preacher, and the same woman did to me, what she did to you. You women in here are not all innocent. Y'all have done some dirty deeds, too. Your sins will truly find you out, you just wait awhile." As he was talking, he looked back at the door and said, "You can't run and you can't hide. God knows where you live." All the men looked at each other and smiled. The women didn't say a word from then on. Reverend Hanns asked James to come forward. He sat a chair in front of the church, and James began to speak, "I have done a bad thing to one of God's children. I went to one of my neighbor's house. There was a young girl in the home. I let the step-momma trick me into going to that child, and now she is going to have my child. I want you all to forgive me for this terrible sin I have committed. I wish I could turn back the hands on the clock, but I can't. You all don't know how bad I feel about this. I just want the church to forgive me. If I don't ever do anything in this church again, just forgive me, please."

One of the women in the church raised her hand and asked, "Are you talking about Mr. Tom's daughter, Clair? I heard some of the young girls in my neighborhood talking about her getting big around the waist. I told them they were lying on that child. She is only about thirteen or fourteen years old. You mean to tell me you messed with a child of her age? James, you are a church man. No woman in hell could have made nobody in this church do that." One of the men in the church looked at the woman and said, "Well, a man in hell made you have two outside children, and you was married to my brother Crawford." Everyone started smiling and whispering to each other. The Reverend had to calm them down. "All right members, let's not go there.

If we start pointing fingers tonight, none of us will be able to hold our heads up tomorrow. We all will have to stay in the house and never show our faces again. So, listen to me. Brother James told us what has happened. Now, we need to talk to the young lady and her family. Can you imagine what is going on with this girl? That whole family needs prayer. If she is showing by now, all of her friends are talking about her. They probably think she's been running around with all the boys in the neighborhood. We are going to take up a love offering on Sunday. Then I will appoint twelve good men to take some food there and give her some money. Brother James, you need to go to the family and tell them you are guilty. Tell them how sorry you are, and then on Sunday, we will all go to the house, and have prayer with the family," said The Reverend.

All of a sudden, an old woman who sat on the corner of the fourth pew stood. She leaned on her walking stick, put one hand on her hip and said, "May I say something before we leave here tonight? I started not to say anything, but I just couldn't hold my peace. I am older than all you members in here. I've been going to church ever since I was a little girl. My grandfather was the founder of this church. I don't go around talking about my brothers and sisters in Christ. I don't try – I live a holy life before man and my God. This ain't the first time a man has done such a deed as this. It's been going on for years. I can tell you stories about church folks that would make you cry. You all forget that there's a God above, and we must answer to him for all we do! God could have stopped James and that old lady right in their tracks, but He allowed it to happen. Put everything in God's hands, He will work it out. You all forgot about love. We must love each other, regardless what happens in our everyday walk. We gonna make mistakes, and we're going to fall, but don't stay in the mud and keep doing wrong. God wakes us up each day. If you do wrong today, go to your brother or sister. Ask for forgiveness, and the next day don't do that sin again. I just had to say something. I don't like to see the church acting this way. I'm ninety years old now. I hope and pray that you all will live as long as I have. And Brother James, I want to leave this with you. Don't ever think of doing what you did to that child again. You better do right about her. If you don't, you know what the scripture says in verses 14 and 15: 'The wicked draw their swords and strings their bows to kill the poor and the oppressed, to slaughter those who do right. But their swords will stab their own hearts, and their bows will be broken.' God's words don't lie."

The Reverend asked everybody to stand and say the watch word together. They departed and went their separate ways. As The Reverend walked to his wagon, he stopped the old lady and thanked her for what she said. Brother James shook everybody's hand, and left in peace.

Chapter Three
Fourth Month

I T WAS THE SEASON FOR COTTON PICKING. Clair was ready to go to the field. She packed her lunch and got on the wagon with her father. "Can I sit on the front with you, Papa?" she asked. Mr. Tom looked at Clair and said, "No, my lady. You need to stay in the back. I don't want you to fall off here. Anyways, you don't need to be a showing off yourself. You need to make some more dresses to wear around."

Clair got on the back of the wagon. She held her head down in shame. She looked at her stomach, and began to trace with her fingers the movement of the child she was carrying. They rode for about four miles to the cotton field. There were other pickers in the field. Some of the people there were friends who attended Clair's church and school. The women who were in the fields stopped picking and watched Clair as she got off the wagon. They stared at her until she got to her appointed rows of cotton. "Clair," her papa yelled. "You get your sack and pick the last four rows. I want them picked by twelve noon." Clair looked at the sun. She looked at the four rows of cotton. She couldn't see the end of either row. She bent her back and began picking as fast as she could. She got down on her knees and crawled to get all the cotton out of the bows. All of a sudden, she dropped to the ground and fell asleep. She slept for about an hour. When her papa got close to where she was, he saw her lying in the field. "My lady, what do mean sleeping on the job? Get up, my lady! Get up before Mr. Winfrey comes!"

Clair got up. She looked in her sack and saw that she only had a half sack of cotton. She had only picked one row. It was already eight o'clock. She had to pick three rows in four hours. She went to her sheet and took a drink of water. She poured some of the water in her face. Finally, she felt better. She started picking as fast as she could. She didn't look up at all. Her fingers began to hurt and cramp up. Her back was hurting from all the bending. She had picked two more rows within an hour. She emptied her sack on the sheet. She was ready to go back where she stopped. By twelve noon, she had completed all four rows of cotton.

Her papa examined her rows. They were all clean! He didn't see any cotton left in the bows. At twelve noon on the dot, he told her to come eat her lunch. After lunch, they picked until six o'clock that evening. Clair was too tired to argue about where she wanted to sit on the wagon. She was just glad to have a place to sit.

When they arrived at home, Mrs. Betsy was sitting in the kitchen. She watched Clair as she walked past the door. "I have some chores for you to do, Missy. Do you hear me talking to you?" she asked Clair.

Clair didn't answer her.

She went to her room and sat on the bed where her sister was lying. "How much cotton did you pick today?" asked Cleo. "I think I picked about five hundred pounds," said Clair. "Papa watched the man weigh it. I was so tired, I just wanted to get home and go to sleep. Did you have a good day today?" Clair asked her sister. "Yes, it was all right. I don't like staying here with Mrs. Betsy. Clair, when you have your baby, I'm going to stay here until the baby is about a month old, and then I'm going to leave here. I'm getting tired of that old woman. I don't know why Papa married her in the first place. We can take care of him and ourselves," Cleo said. Clair lay on the bed with her feet on top of the covers. She folded her arms underneath her breasts. She was watching the cracks in the ceiling, and she answered her sister, "Sis, you know Papa needs a woman to keep him happy, do you know what I mean? Every man needs a woman in the home, especially when there are children like us with no momma. Mrs. Betsy been with us for ten years now, and Papa ain't putting her out. So we have to deal with her until we are able to leave. This is our home. If she doesn't do right, Papa will put her in her place," said Clair.

Cleo raised herself up to look at Clair, and said, "So what is he going to do about Mr. James and what he did to you? Our Pa ain't no church-going man, but he lives better than some of those men who stay in the church every Sunday. I can't ever remember Papa hurting nobody. He treats everybody right. He teaches us how to pray, and he lets us go to church with Aunt Allie. He wants us to do what is right. I don't know why he walks around the house and says, the Lord is gonna fix it. Do you think he believes in God, Clair?" Clair looked at Cleo. Then she put her arms around her sister and said, "I know Papa is a good man, and I believe he fears God. I can tell when we have a bad storm. He always tells us to sit down and don't say a word, 'cause God is talking to us through the storm. One night, I was in the barn putting the rake up. I saw Papa sitting in the loft. He didn't see me. I heard him talking to God. He was crying and he had the bible in his hand. He was acting like some of the people at church when they get happy in the Spirit. I walked out so he wouldn't see me. I know he wishes Momma was here sometimes."

Cleo looked at Clair and asked, "Do you remember what Momma looked like, Clair?" Clair looked at Cleo with tears in her eyes and said, "A little bit. I was only three years old when she left us and you was just born. She was beautiful. She had long hair and she was white looking, just like us." Cleo looked at her arms and asked, "Are we white, Clair?" Clair wiped her eyes and answered, "No. And don't you let Pa hear you say that. Our momma had a hard time when she was growing up. I heard Papa say her daddy was a white man. Our grandma worked for a white family. They lived on the man's farm, and Grandma lived in the house with the family. Our grandma must have been a pretty woman, too. Don't let Papa know I told you this story, so you keep it to yourself, for life. You hear what I said?"

Cleo turned over in the bed and fell asleep. Clair got up to take a bath. She looked down the hallway to see if Papa and Mrs. Betsy were still up. She didn't see a light on, so she prepared herself for bed.

The next morning, Clair got up early as usual. She didn't have to work in the field today, so she decided to go into town. She wanted to walk this day, because she needed to get out and have some time to herself. It took her about an hour to get to where she needed to go. She saw some of the girls who went to school with her. One of the girls who was in her school didn't like Clair. She would call Clair names, and made her feel bad about herself in front of the other girls. As Clair walked by, that girl started singing a made up song: "Brown, get down; white, you're all right; black, get back; yellow, go down town and get you a fellow." She repeated it over and over again. Clair pretended they were not there. "How many fellows have you had, yellow gal?" the girl asked disrespectfully. Clair didn't say anything to them. She just kept walking until she got inside the store. The girls followed Clair into the store. "Oh, my God, she's going to have a baby!" One of the girls said, "I wonder! Who's the daddy? Or better than that, does she know who the daddy is?" another girl asked. Clair paid the clerk for her goods and left the store. She didn't look back. As she walked across the street, one of the women from the church was watching the girls who were talking to Clair. "Come here, child," she said. "Are you all right? Do you need anything, honey? I heard those girls making fun of you. Don't you worry about them! They are going to get what's coming to them later in life. You just watch and see. I've never seen the righteous forsaken, nor His seed begging for bread. You're a good girl, and don't you let nobody tell you anything different. God is going to take care of you. You keep your head up. Do you hear what I'm saying, child?" the woman said.

Clair thanked the woman, and went on her way. She held the bags close to her chest, and wondered, *"Why they have to talk about my skin? I didn't make myself yellow. I was born like this. Half white! You so yellow! Your momma is a white woman! On and on, they always talk about Cleo and me. If we could do something about it, then we would. If we were black as a tar baby, they would have something to say about that, too. I don't care what they say anymore. I am who*

I am, and that's that!"

Chapter Four
Seventh Month

THE COTTON SEASON WAS ALMOST OVER. School was beginning for the fall, except for Clair. At seven months pregnant, she had to stay at home, help on the farm and take care of the house. She was ashamed to go into town to get rations for the house. Papa told her to stay close to home, because he was afraid she would have the child early.

Clair began cleaning her room. She took old clothes out of the boxes that were packed during the winter. It was time to wash and clean her sweaters and the other clothes for Cleo and the boys. Mrs. Betsy stood in the hallway. She put her hands on her hips and said, "Why you taking all those clothes out of your room? You're not going anywhere, Missy. Just put them back and come in here and help with the dinner." Clair continued to go through the boxes. She didn't want anything to do with Mrs. Betsy.

All of a sudden, Mrs. Betsy walked up to the box and kicked it over. Clair stood up and gave Mrs. Betsy a look that would almost kill a person. "Why did you do that? I'm taking these clothes out to wash and fold for the winter!" screamed Clair. "Touch them again and I'll throw them out the door and burn them!" Mrs. Betsy shouted back. Clair began to cry. Her feelings were getting the best of her. "I don't know why you're so mean to me. I don't bother anybody. Day after day, you always picking a fight with me. What have I done to you so bad, that you treat me this way? I don't do nothing to nobody! It's always me! Tell me, Mrs. Betsy! Why? Why? Why?" Clair screamed as she covered her ears.

Mrs. Betsy looked at Clair as if she was having a fit. She stepped back in fear. She didn't know whether she wanted to run first or scream for help. She slowly backed down the hallway. She watched Clair as she walked into her room. She closed the door and locked the latch. Clair picked up all the clothes that were on the floor. Tears ran down her cheeks. She wiped her face, but the tears would not stop flowing. She placed the clothes on a chair near the kitchen.

Meanwhile, Cleo was outside playing with the neighborhood kids. She stopped and stared at the house. There was shouting coming from inside. She ran to the kitchen door and asked, "What's going on in here? What's wrong with you, Clair? Did she hurt you? Clair, answer me! I'm going to tell Papa."

Mr. Tom was in the field plowing with his mule. He heard Cleo yelling. He stopped and looked toward the house. Cleo was running as if there was a fire. She grabbed her papa's legs and cried, "Papa, I'm not sure, but there's something wrong with Clair. I heard Mrs. Betsy and

Clair fussing at each other. She made Clair cry." Mr. Tom hugged Cleo and told her that everything was going to be all right. He explained to her that women folk would have it out at times. He loosed the mule from the plow and walked Cleo back to the house.

When he arrived at the yard, Clair was sitting on the swing. "My lady, what's wrong with you and Betsy in here?" Clair began to cry again. Cleo looked at her, to see if she was going to say something. "Do you hear me talking to you, lady?" Clair just shook her head, as if to say there was nothing wrong.

Mr. Tom walked into the house. He looked for Mrs. Betsy. He walked to the kitchen, then the bedroom, and found her sitting on the bed. "Why you keep at this girl, Betsy? Haven't you done enough damage here? If it don't stop, I'm gon' put you out my house. I didn't bring you here to treat my children bad. If you don't love them, just leave them alone! I can beat them, love them, and scold them all by myself. I don't need a woman of your kind staying here. If it keeps on happening, you can just get on out of here. You hear me talking to you?" asked Mr. Tom.

Mrs. Betsy remained silent. She just sat on the bed and stared at Mr. Tom. Finally, he left the room. He thought, *"That's a mean old woman. Lord, why in the world did I put that woman in here with my family? I thought I was doing right. That's right, Lord, I didn't ask you about her."* Then he walked outside and sat on the porch with Cleo and Clair.

Chapter Five
Ninth Month

REVEREND HANNS VISITED MR. TOM'S HOME EVERY WEEK. The church collected money for Clair and the family. The pastor always sent one of the deacons to take the offering and dry goods to the house. But on this fourth Sunday in October, he asked Brother James to take the offering. The Reverend stopped James as he was leaving the church. "Brother, I want you to take the offering to Mr. Tom's house today. You think your wife will go with you?" the pastor asked. James looked down at the ground, and said he didn't know. He turned his head and looked away off, and said, "I'll ask her, but if she says no, I'll take it myself." The Pastor hesitated for a moment and said, "Listen to me, I know this is asking a lot of you, but you got to forgive yourself first, before others can forgive you. If your family and friends see how this is affecting you, they will never stop talking about this thing. Let it go, and be the man God wants you to be. You got to confess to God. Be sincere with your confession. You don't want to be an enemy to God. He says in His word the wicked will die. The Lord's enemies are like flowers in a field — they will disappear like smoke. You will stop feeling guilty, and you will become a godly man."

Reverend Hanns put his hand on James' shoulder and continued, "The Lord directs the steps of the godly brother, James. He delights in every detail of their lives. Though they stumble, they will never fall, for the Lord holds them by the hand. Just remember these words, my brother. This too, will pass. Just hold on and don't never stop praying."

James shook The Reverend's hand and thanked him. "I'll take the rations and the money. I need to talk to Clair by myself," James said. "She gonna have the child in about three more weeks, I hear. I've been a church man too long, Reverend. I need to really forgive myself. I go to church every Sunday. I'm just like the seeds the farmer sowed by the wayside. I was thrown too close to the wayside. Something is always going on in my life. I get distracted by any little thing. I should be listening to you on Sunday mornings and Wednesday nights, but I let any old thing take me off the Word of God. I believe something is going to happen to me soon or later, and that something in my life is going to shake me up. And then, I'll be all right. I just hope it won't be too late," said James.

James went home to ask Mrs. Elisha to go with him to take the money and food. As he entered the house, Mrs. Elisha asked, "James, is that you?" "Yes. Do you have anything to do this evening?" asked James. "No, I don't. Why?" Mrs. Elisha asked. "The Pastor asked me to take some money that the church raised for the poor to the homes today, and I want to know if you want to go with me?" he asked. James didn't hear her answer. He looked in the kitchen. Mrs. Elisha was standing at the stove. "Did you hear me, Elisha?" he asked. Mrs. Elisha continued to stir the food in the pot. "Why you want me to go with you?" she asked. James sat down at the table. "Elisha, we need to talk about this here thing. You haven't said much to me about it. I need to know your thoughts about this child that is being born next month. Please, come sit down here, and let's talk. Please!" pleaded James.

Mrs. Elisha sat down at the table. James held her hand. "You know, I been praying to God. I talked to my Pastor and friends at the church, but I didn't think about you and your feelings about all of this. I need to know something. Will you please forgive me? I really want to be forgiven by God, and I need to be forgiven by you. This thing has truly worried me, ever since it happened. We haven't been close in about a year now. Just let me know your feelings about all of this. If for some reason you can't forgive me, I can understand that. But tell me what you think!" begged James.

Mrs. Elisha looked at James and said, "You know, James. That was a bad thing you did to that child. Knowing we have a daughter, too, I just can't seem to put it behind me. It happened and it ain't nothing nobody can do about it but God. I don't want you to take nothing from this family for that child. You hear me, James?" asked Elisha. "You have always worked and provided for us, and that better not stop. You do for that gal now, but when that baby comes here, it's gonna be up to her family to deal with that. I forgive it, but who told me I had to forget it?" Elisha asked.

James looked at Mrs. Elisha with tears in his eyes. "I hear what you're saying. I'll keep my family up. I can take on another job. I'll start selling off my old wagon," said James.

James got up from the table. He walked out with his head down. Then he came back to the kitchen door and asked, "Does that mean you're going with me this evening?" Mrs. Elisha looked at him and said, "Yes, but I'm not going in the house! I'll stay on the wagon with my children."

The weather was changing. The leaves filled the yards as far as the eye could see. Clair stayed in the house now more than ever before. Cleo was going to school with her brothers. Mr. Tom worked the fields for several farmers in that county. He hated to leave Clair at home by herself. He tried to get Mrs. Betsy to help on the farms with him, but she refused to work outside the house. He knew the time was coming soon for Clair to have her baby. One moment he would pray to himself and ask the Lord to bless the child's coming in and going out. Then, he would feel sorry for the child. The baby was coming into a world of sin. He didn't want anything to happen to it.

It was going to be his first grandchild! That made him happy inside. All of a sudden, he stopped what he was doing and knelt down to pray. *"Father, our Father who is in Heaven. Glory be Your name. Lord, You know me. This is Tom. I love You Lord, and always will. I'm not a church man, Father, but I love You, Lord. I try to obey You at everything I do. I get up early in the morning and give thanks for everything You do for me. That's not enough, Lord. I need to do more. I know Your Word is true. I believe every word in Your holy book. Lord, don't leave me, and don't take Your hands off my little children. Bless everybody in this world and the world that's coming after me. Bless this little child who is coming in this world of sin. Don't let nobody take her life but You, Lord. Let her grow to be a blessing to You. Let her always pray for guidance, and lead her into the path of righteousness for Your name's sake. And when the shadow of death comes, let her fear no evil. I ask all these blessings in your Holy name, Jesus,"* Mr. Tom prayed.

Mr. Tom stood and brushed off his knees. He looked at the sun. He got on his wagon and headed for home. When he arrived at home, he walked into the house. Clair was in her room. The church members had brought her some things for the new baby. She placed the things in a pile near the foot of her bed. Mr. Tom walked to her door, and said, "My lady, are you all right today?" He sat down on the bed, and folded his hands. "Do you need anything?" he asked. Clair put her head on his shoulder, and said, "I'm scared, Papa. I don't know what's going to happen to me. I don't know how to have this baby. I want to have it, and then I don't. I am so scared, Papa."

Mr. Tom stood up, and said, "I know what I can do. I'll go get your momma's sister, Allie. She's good with you girls. She always comes on Wednesdays anyhow, but I'll talk to her this week. God knows all about His children. Don't you worry yourself none."

Chapter Six
Neighborhood News

November 12, 1932

CLAIR WAS AT HOME WASHING THE CLOTHES FOR THE FAMILY. Cleo and the boys were raking the yard. Mrs. Betsy had to go into town with Mr. Tom. Aunt Allie rode up to the house in a wagon. Her sons were with her. They helped her off the wagon. She walked to the house, and asked the children for Clair. They told her that Clair was in the house hanging the clothes near the fireplace. She walked into the house and yelled, "Clair, you in here? Where you at, child?" Clair dropped everything, and ran to the front room. They hugged each other tightly. Aunt Allie felt Clair's stomach, and said, "You gon' have this baby soon. I mean real soon, honey! It may come tonight, or sometime tomorrow. Don't you be going nowhere, and don't lift nothing heavy. You hear me, Clair?"

Aunt Allie said her goodbyes to the children and rode into town. She went to her favorite place in the store. She traded some eggs for a boat of new material. She had to make dresses for Leslie and Carrie. She decided to make an extra dress for Clair. On her way out, she saw three of her church members. The three women spoke to Aunt Allie. "Allie, I don't mean to gossip, but has that child of Tom's had that baby yet?" one of the women asked. Aunt Allie put her hands on her hips and gave that woman a look from way back when, and said, "Why you asking me about that child? Don't you live near Tom? Why didn't you ask him about her? That's his child. She ain't mine!"

The woman didn't know what to say. The other lady who was with the woman grabbed her arm and told her to come on. "That Allie has always been a mess," said the lady. "She's just like her daddy. They will get you told and don't mind doing it. Somebody told me when her boys go out on the town and come home late, she makes them sleep in the tobacco barn. She don't allow them to come in her house with liquor on they breath. That woman is something else. The whole neighborhood knows about the girl. They can't keep it a secret. My daughter said she's been big for a long time. It's about time for the baby to be born, if it ain't already here!" she said.

The women left the store. Aunt Allie got on her wagon and headed toward home. On their way, one of the boys asked, "Ma, how in the world is Clair gon' raise a baby in that house? Somebody needs to stay with her and make sure she is all right. Uncle Tom works all the time, and the boys are young. They need some help there. Is Mrs. Betsy still there, Ma?" Aunt Allie just prayed to herself as the boys guided the wagon. She was a good Christian woman, and she didn't take no mess from the people in the neighborhood. "Well, James got that child pregnant," said Aunt Allie. "He ain't no bad man, and then he ain't no good man either. The devil can get into anybody, even you boys. But you better not let me hear of it. You better leave these old gals alone!" Aunt Allie said. "Don't take nothing from them – no chewing gum, no candy, and don't drink after them. These gals will put something on stuff and make you love them. You will be messed up for life. Don't y'all never go with a girl who runs after you. They won't make you a good wife. You go see the girl, and leave her house before it gets dark. Have respect for yourself. If you don't do like I say, you gon' have a hard time with these women. Look at poor Tom. He wishes many a day he would have left Betsy where she was," Aunt Allie said.

Late that night, Aunt Allie saw a light outside her bedroom window. She heard a knock on their door. Aunt Allie got out of bed. She went to the door and asked who it was. "It's me. Tom. Let me in!" said Mr. Tom. "You got to come with me. I think Clair is having her child. She's been in bed all day, and she's in a lot of pain. I told Betsy to watch her until I get back, and that old woman won't get out the bed," said Mr. Tom. Aunt Allie put her coat and hat on. She told the girls that she had to go with Mr. Tom. The boys got up and went with Aunt Allie.

Aunt Allie stayed at Mr. Tom's house until daybreak. Clair was about to have the baby. Mr. Tom was on his way to get the doctor. It took about thirty minutes to go to town and back. Around noon, Clair delivered a seven pound baby girl. Aunt Allie was so proud of Clair. She took the baby in her arms so that Clair could get some sleep. Mr. Tom looked at the baby and said, "What a fine baby girl!" Then he went to the barn and got some of his old quilts. He hung them over the window so the daylight wouldn't hurt the baby's eyes. He placed extra quilts on Clair, and asked her if she was all right.

Aunt Allie sat in the old rocking chair near Clair's bed and said, "Clair, what be this child's name?" Clair looked at Aunt Allie and said, "I want to name her Olivia. I saw that name in a catalog at the general store. Do you have another name for her, Aunt Allie?" Aunt Allie held the baby up to light and said, "That's a pretty name for this young'un. Do you know how to care for the baby, Clair?" Clair nodded, then rolled over in the bed and fell asleep.

Aunt Allie put the baby in a box that Tom had made for her. She then dressed the baby in warm clothes and a light blanket that she had made. She gathered her things and told the boys that they had to go. Tom thanked Aunt Allie and the boys for coming. Clair stayed in bed all day long. When the baby cried, she tried nursing her. It was hard for her to get the baby to nurse, but the baby finally latched on.

Clair got up the next morning and washed herself and her baby. She opened the box that the church had given her for the baby. She dressed the baby and put her back to bed. Later that evening, Mrs. Betsy went to Clair's room and said, "Let me see that baby, gal." Clair didn't say a word. She uncovered the child and showed her to Mrs. Betsy. "Did Allie name her?" she asked Clair. "No, I named my own baby," Clair said confidently. "Well, don't think you gonna stay in this bed all day. We got work to do in this here house. You been lying around for days, and it's time to let that baby sleep and you get up and do something," Mrs. Betsy demanded. Clair didn't say a word. She stayed in her room and nursed her newborn baby.

Cleo and the boys came home from school. They were excited to see the baby. The boys asked Clair if there was something they could do for her. Cleo did Clair's chores, so she could tend to the baby. Mr. Tom was in the field with his mule and plow, but he had to keep an eye on Mrs. Betsy. She didn't like Clair, and she sure didn't like that she had a new baby.

Weeks went by and the baby was now a month old. It seemed that Mr. Tom and Betsy would argue more than ever. It was always about something that Clair wasn't doing. Aunt Allie usually visited Clair on Wednesday evenings and Sunday afternoons, but she didn't come this Wednesday. Clair didn't know what happened. She got up as usual, did her work in the house, and gathered the clothes to wash. She went to the well and drew water for the kitchen while the baby slept.

Mrs. Betsy was in her room reading. She called Clair, and asked her to go outside and get some wood for the heater. Clair got her coat and scarf. She went outside to cut small pieces of wood with the ax. Mrs. Betsy watched her as she cut the wood. Then she went back inside the house. She went to Clair's room and found the baby asleep in Clair's bed. Mrs. Betsy took the heavy quilt and covered the baby's whole body. The baby couldn't move or breathe. Mrs. Betsy ran to the door, and called Clair and said, "Come here Clair, I got something to show you!" Clair dropped the ax and ran to the house. Mrs. Betsy stood in the doorway to block Clair from coming in. Clair asked what was wrong. "Go in there and look at your baby," she said. Clair ran to her room. The baby was under the quilt. She wasn't moving. Clair threw the quilt off the baby, and saw that she wasn't breathing either. Clair grabbed the baby and ran to the kitchen where the water pail was. She took a handful of water and poured it on the baby's face. The baby began to scream uncontrollably. Clair held her baby tight to her chest and cried. She walked back to her room. She sat in the old rocking chair and nursed her baby. Mrs. Betsy just stood in the door staring out at the chickens in the yard. The plan she had for the baby didn't work out.

Later that night, Clair told Mr. Tom what had happened to her baby. He sat down and cried as she told her story. "Your Aunt Allie is coming Sunday, and I want you to talk to her about this thing," said Mr. Tom. "I don't want nothing to happen to you or the baby. You girls are old enough to take care of yourselves now. I need to let that old woman go on her way. She ain't nothing but trouble in my house. I have had a hard time raising you children. The Lord let me see my first grandchild, and I want to live to see some more," Mr. Tom cried.

On Sunday evening, Aunt Allie left the church and went to see Clair and the baby. Clair was sitting on the front porch with the baby in her arms. She saw the wagon coming down the road. She got up to see if it was Aunt Allie. Clair smiled and thought, *"I knew she would come! I'm going to tell her everything. She's the only one who can get Mrs. Betsy straight."*

Aunt Allie stopped the wagon in front of the house. "Hey, Baby. How are you two doing today?" she asked. "I brought some chicken and potato pies with me. Big meeting was today, and the people had more food than they could eat, so I told them to pack some of it up, and I'll take it Tom's house. So here we are!" Aunt Allie said. Clair held her head down as if she was worried about something. She held her baby even tighter and looked at Aunt Allie and said, "I need to talk to you about something. Let's go in my room. I don't want Mrs. Betsy to hear me."

They walked into the house. Clair led Aunt Allie to her room. Aunt Allie sat on the bed and reached for the baby. Clair told her what Mrs. Betsy did. She cried as she recalled what happened. When she finished talking, Aunt Allie told her to pack the baby's things and have her ready to go with her on Wednesday. If she didn't let her go, sooner or later, Mrs. Betsy was going to kill the baby. Clair told her papa what Aunt Allie said, and he agreed.

On that next Wednesday, Aunt Allie came to the house just as she had promised. She had all her children with her. Carrie took the baby from Clair and got on the wagon. As they rode off, Clair knelt down to the ground and cried. She loved her baby, but she wanted her to live and have a good life someday. Aunt Allie was just the right person who could make that dream come true.

Olivia was the baby in the family. They loved her dearly. She grew to be a beautiful little girl. They took her everywhere they went. They celebrated her birthdays, took her to the church meetings, and visited her mother on different occasions.

Soon Olivia was school age. Carrie worked with her during the summer to help prepare her for school. Olivia was shy and didn't know how to act with children her own age. She had to learn to share and be considerate of others. Carrie would talk to her about the rules at school. "Olivia, when you go to school, you have to obey your teacher. She won't be like Ma. You can't sit in her lap. You can't go to sleep in class, or eat in class. You have to ask for permission before you do any-thing. Do you hear me?"

Olivia looked at Carrie and answered, "Yes. I know!"

Chapter Seven
First Day of School

September 6, 1937

SCHOOL WAS ABOUT TO OPEN. Aunt Allie had to take Olivia to the pre-school day. She was excited to go to school.

The next week was the first day of school. Olivia learned to read and write. She especially loved recess. She learned to get along with the other girls in her class. She always remembered what Aunt Allie – whom she called "Ma" – told her, "Don't talk back to older people, and you'd better not fight other children." Aunt Allie wanted her to be a good girl when she wasn't around, because Carrie and the other children had spoiled her. She was the baby in the house, and the other children were older than she was. They would give her whatever she wanted when they got a chance.

One day, while Olivia was playing at school, a strange man came to the school house fence. When he got closer, he called Olivia and said, "Come here, baby. I got something for you." Olivia walked over to the fence. The man gave her two dollars and told her not to tell Betty and Jimmy. Olivia thanked him, and ran back to play with the other children. She looked at the money and put it in her dress pocket. When she got home that evening, she told Aunt Allie what the man did and gave her the money. Aunt Allie looked at Olivia and said, "I bet that was Ol' James. I know how he is, always searching around for something." Olivia looked at her and asked, "Ma, who is James?"

Aunt Allie didn't want to lie. She told Olivia that James was her real daddy. She told her that James was married and had two children, Betty and Jimmy. "Pa is your daddy, too," said Aunt Allie as she dressed Olivia for bed. "And Clair is your real momma. I just took you when you was a little baby. Your momma was only fourteen when she had you. Her momma was dead. Somebody had to take over, 'cause your Grandpa, Tom, was a little slow." She told Lessie that she was getting up early in the morning. She had to go and pay that James a visit. When Aunt Allie said something, she meant it. She didn't take no wooden nickels from nobody.

That next Saturday evening, Aunt Allie told the boys to load up the wagon with everything she needed. She rode for about an hour to James' house. When she got there, she saw his wife, Mrs. Elisha, hanging out clothes on the line. Betty and Jimmy were playing in the back yard. She got off the wagon, and walked to the clothes line. "How you do today, Elisha?" Aunt Allie asked. "I don't mean to bother you this here morning, but I want to talk to James. Is he here?" Aunt Allie asked. Mrs. Elisha stopped what she was doing, and looked at Aunt Allie, and said, "Yes'um. What you need with him?" Aunt Allie was about to say one thing and another came out. "He went to the school to see my baby. I want him to stay away from her. He's done enough damage for a life time. Is he here?" she asked again.

James was in the barn. He heard someone talking. He came from the barn to see who it was. He knew Aunt Allie from the church. He walked toward Aunt Allie and said, "Yes'um Mrs. Allie, can I help you with something?" She turned around and saw James standing next to her, and said, "James, my baby said you came by the school last week. Did you give her some money? 'Cause, if you did, we don't need nothing from you. You disowned this child when her momma got her from you. You done did enough to that family. I mean for you to say away from her." Aunt Allie said her peace and walked to the wagon. James was at a loss for words. He was ashamed, because Mrs. Elisha was standing there to hear every word said. He said nothing to his wife and she said nothing in return.

James got on his wagon and rode into town. He saw The Reverend at the church and stopped to chat. Reverend Hanns greeted James and asked was everything all right. James began to tell him what happened. "Brother James, you need to confess your sins to everybody," said The Reverend. "That woman thinks you are the same old sinful man you was before you confessed at church. Have you tried to talk to her before today?" he asked. James put his hands in his pocket and said, "No sir, I haven't. I should have gone to the house to see my child when I heard she had her. I'm trying to keep peace in my home. Elisha wants me to work all the time and give her all the money. I guess she thinks I'm going to give Clair and the baby something," he said.

"I got another job now," James continued. "I sell little snacks on the road when I sell wood. I plan to get some household goods and sell them, too. I'm trying, Reverend. I want to do what's right. I'm going to Mrs. Allie's house and tell her just how I feel. If I have to go down on all fours, that's what I'll do." The Reverend told James that was the right thing do. And by doing that, God would bless him and his household. "I want to leave this with you my friend," said The Reverend. "Once I was young, and now I am old. Yet, I have never seen the godly abandoned or their children begging for bread. The godly always give generous loans to others, and their children are a blessing," said The Reverend.

James thanked The Reverend for his encouraging words. As James walked toward his wagon, he prayed, *"Lord, I have always been in the church, but the church wasn't in me. I don't want the name of being a church man. I want to be a man of God. If You, Lord, forgive me, and I go and ask the people whom I have hurt to forgive me, then, Lord, I think I can travel this here road until You come for me. Lord, give my enemies the heart to forgive me, and I will forever serve You and only You. I confess all my sins to You, Lord. I slept with the deacons' wives. I stole some money from the church one time. I put it back, but I still stole it. I looked at my neighbor's daughters. I didn't touch them, but I still looked. I was wrong! I talked ugly to my wife. She's a good woman and she tried to tell me when I was wrong. It was me all the time. I didn't want to listen to her, because she was right! And Lord, this last thing I'm going to say. I didn't read my bible like I should have. I pretended I was reading it. I would fall asleep and I lied to The Reverend. I would tell him I read the entire chapter, when I knew I didn't. Please forgive me, Lord. Please Lord! Lord! I'm so sorry!"*

James wiped the tears from his eyes as he went down the road.

Chapter Eight
Half-Brothers and Sisters

MRS. ELISHA WAS A PROUD LITTLE WOMAN. She always dressed her children with the best clothes in the store. James was doing well at selling his household goods. He bought a used truck from one of the white farmers in town. Everything was going well with him and his family.

One day, Betty was talking to some of her friends at school. One of the girls who lived near her pulled her aside and asked, "Betty, I heard some of the other girls talking yesterday. They said you have a half-sister. Is that right?" Betty looked at her and turned her nose up, and walked away. The girls talked about Betty and what they had heard. Another girl said, "My mama told me Betty's ma and pa think they are something on a stick! They have a truck and he sells wood, too. She said Betty don't wear nothing but made dresses from the store. Every day, she wears different-colored hair bows, and different-colored socks. I don't know if I have any half-brothers and sisters, but if I did, I think I could love them like my own sister and brother."

Another girl asked, "How do you get a half-sister or brother?" The third girl said, "I guess when your mama or daddy goes out and gets a baby from another woman. That's what Mr. James did. I heard my daddy talking to my mama about it. Do y'all know Olivia's real mom?" The girls gossiped as they walked home from school. They saw Betty's brother, Jimmy. They decided to ask Jimmy about his half-sister, Olivia. "Hello, Jimmy. One of us wants to know do you know your half-sister, Olivia?" Jimmy looked at them and rolled his eyes. He was a stuck-up acting young man. He never said a word; he just gave them an ugly look. "Well, I guess he told us!" one of the girls said.

Those girls decided to go on home and leave Betty and Jimmy alone. They tried to get it started, but it didn't work out like they thought it would.

Betty didn't have a lot of friends, because she wasn't a friendly girl herself. She always sat by herself at church every Sunday and Wednesday night. Her momma didn't associate with the other women in the church either. It was noticeable. The other women in the church would get together and cook dinner for Reverend Hanns and his wife, but not Mrs. Elisha. She knew the women were talking about James and what he did, so she stayed to herself, and she didn't want her children sitting with the other children.

The Reverend always said in his reading, "I have seen the wicked and ruthless people flourishing like a tree in its native soil. But when I looked again, they were gone! Though I searched for them, I could not find them!"

Mrs. Elisha is on her high horse now, but in due season, she will need those same people she was ignoring.

Chapter Nine
The Lord Will Fix Everything

"THE LORD RESCUES THE GODLY; HE IS THEIR FORTRESS IN TIMES OF TROUBLE. The Lord helps them, rescuing them from the wicked. He saves them, and they find shelter in Him."

It was a wicked thing that James did to Clair. He confessed his sins to God and to man. But after confessing, he also needed to love everybody.

Confession cleans the soul, and loving everybody prevents the soul from getting dirty again. Our natural bodies crave for many things. However, we must be careful what we feed it. Our eyes and ears are the pathway to our souls. Whatever we meditate on, we allow that thing to enter our soul. So, we must be careful about our emotions, our will, and our mind and not let them get the best of us. Meditate on God's word. The more we do this, the more we will focus on His word, and His word will be food for us.

James confessed his sins. God blessed him for doing so. Mrs. Elisha never accepted Olivia as James' daughter, nor did her children.

Clair married and had four other children. When her husband died, she and James became best friends. He would go by her house to see if they needed anything. He would bring food and wood to her family. He was a businessman in that neighborhood for many years.

Olivia grew tall and beautiful. She married a wonderful man, and they were blessed with ten children, 28 grandchildren, and the great grandchildren are still coming.

James died when Olivia's second child was born. Clair lived to see all of her grandchildren by Olivia.

Olivia is still living with nine of her children. God has truly blessed her for being so obedient to Him.

Just wait on God. He will fix everything that was done wrong in your life.

Wait, I say, on the Lord.

www.ingramcontent.com/pod-product-compliance
Lightning Source LLC
Chambersburg PA
CBHW071345130626
46556CB00005B/2039